This Walker book belongs to:

. . . .

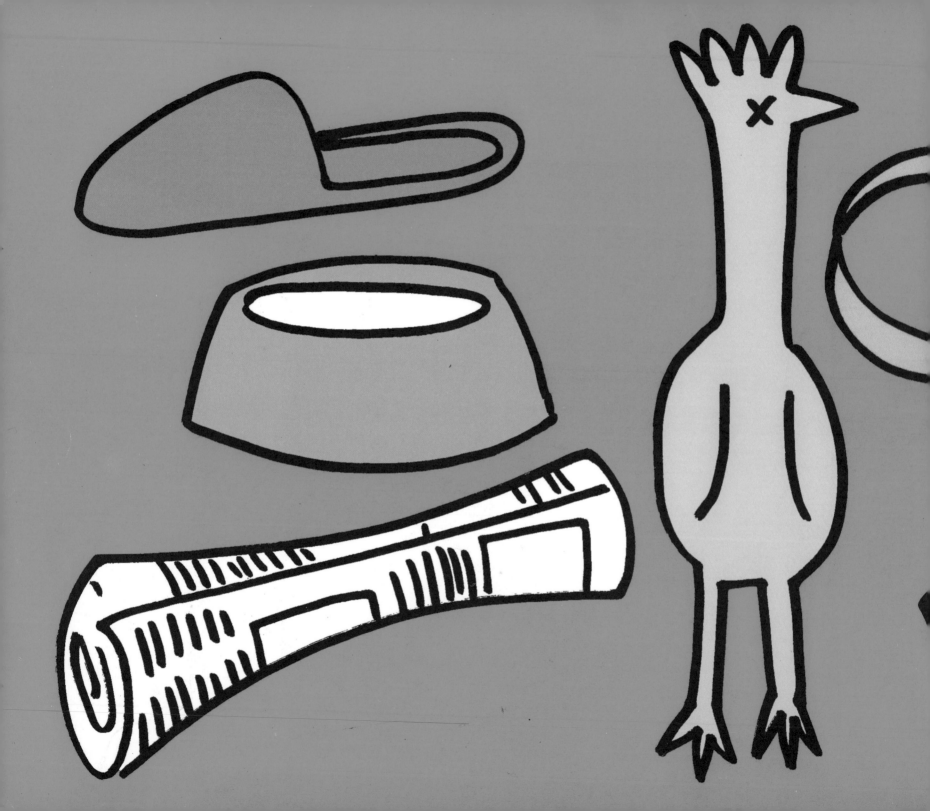

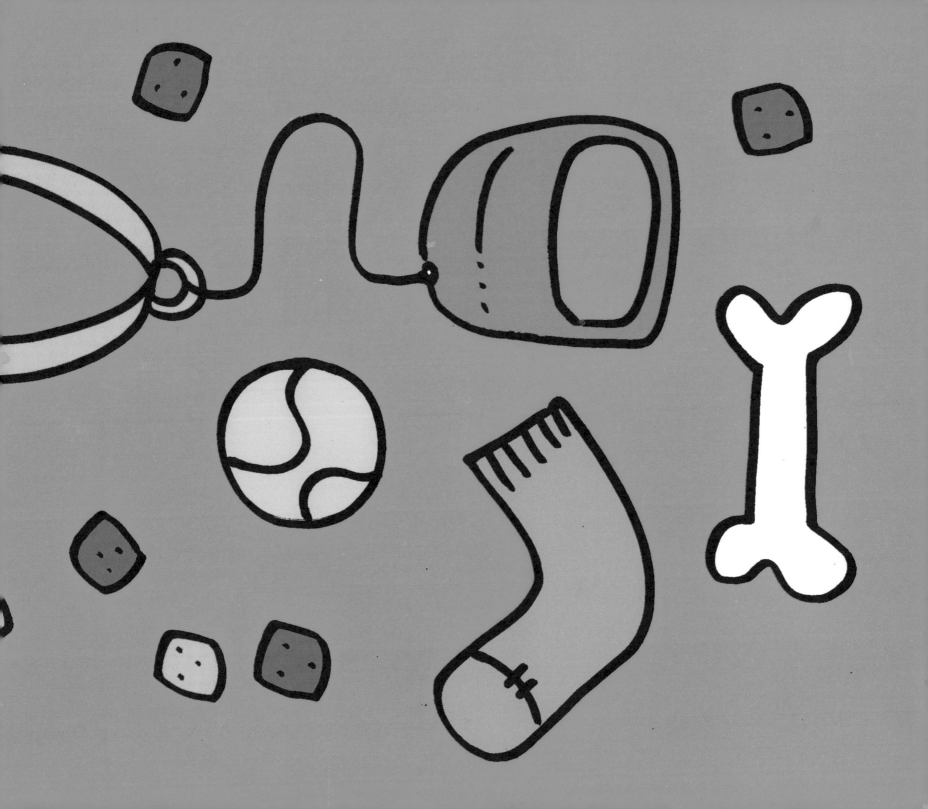

The Dog Book

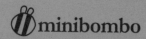 minibombo

First published 2017 by Walker Books Ltd, 87 Vauxhall Walk, London SE11 5HJ • This edition published 2019 • Copyright © 2013 minibombo/TIWI s.r.l. • English language translation © 2017 Walker Books Ltd • First published 2013 by minibombo, Italy as *Il libro cane* by Lorenzo Clerici • Published in the English language by arrangement with minibombo, an imprint of TIWI s.r.l., Via Emilia San Pietro, 25, 42121 Reggio Emilia, Italy • minibombo is a trademark of TIWI s.r.l. © 2013 minibombo/TIWI s.r.l. The moral rights of the author have been asserted • This book has been typeset in Tisa Pro Regular and Medium • Printed in China
• British Library Cataloguing in Publication Data: a catalogue record for this book is available from the British Library • ISBN 978-1-4063-8416-1 • www.walker.co.uk • 10 9 8 7 6 5 4 3 2 1

WALKER BOOKS
AND SUBSIDIARIES
LONDON • BOSTON • SYDNEY • AUCKLAND

FSC
www.fsc.org
MIX
Paper from
responsible sources
FSC™ C020056

Check out **www.minibombo.com**
to find plenty of fun ideas for playing
and creating – all inspired by this book!

I'll call my dog:

. . . .

Zzz zzz

Look at your dog sleeping ...
and listen to him snoring!
Hey, sleepyhead,
it's time to get up!
Do you want to help wake him?
Call out his name
and then turn the page.

Woof!

Yes, you've done it!
Good morning, dozy dog!
Why don't you give him a good
scratch on his back?

Zzz zzz

Oh! What happened?
He's asleep again!
Quick, quick,
give him a shout,
give him a shake,
and then turn the page.

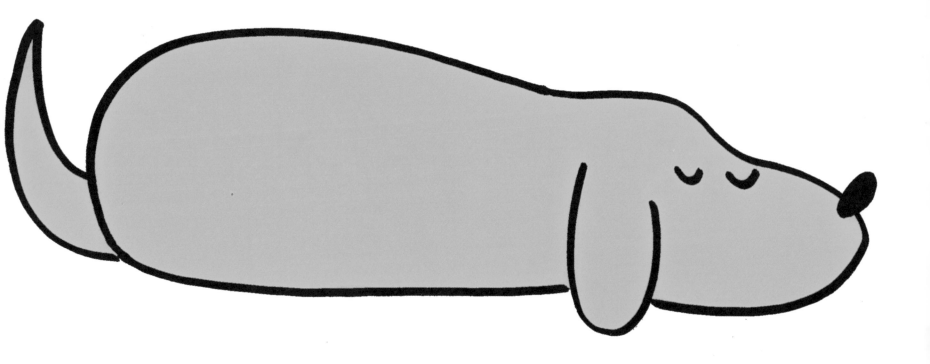

Finally! He's wide awake.
Look how he's wagging his tail!
He wants you to pet him.
Go on, give him a rub.
A *rub rub rub* right on his belly.

Ahhh ... your dog loves it!
But he can't roll around
all day long!
Let's see how well he's trained.
Try telling him to sit
and then turn the page.

Hmm ... he's still sprawling.
Didn't you tell him to sit?
Let's try again.
Ask your dog to sit.

Well done!
He's sitting! He's sitting!
Give him a pat on the head
and tell him, "Good dog."

Oh dear...
He's got quite an itch.
Scratch, dog. Scratch.
Now let's play fetch.
With your finger,
toss the little red ball.

Hmm, where's that ball?
And where's your dog?
Call for him to come back.
Shout his name and say,
"Come on! Come on!"

Phew! There he is.
And he's fetched the ball, too.
But he's so messy and muddy!
Use your shirt to get him clean.

Good job – he's spotless!
But now he's pretty tired.
It's been quite a busy day, after all.
Wish him a good night with a
little tickle under his chin.

Then slowly, so very slowly,
turn the page.

Shhh!

He's asleep.
Good night, dozy dog.
Sleep tight.

Discover more minibombo books!

978-1-4063-6316-6

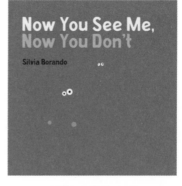

978-1-4063-6317-3

978-1-4063-6421-7

978-1-4063-6318-0

978-1-4063-6733-1

978-1-4063-6734-8

978-1-4063-7214-4

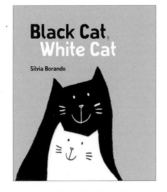

978-1-4063-6744-7

Available from all good booksellers

www.walker.co.uk